TABLE OF CONTENTS

1. Play Safe Outdoors   4

2. Protect Your Body   6

3. Stay Safe around Animals 10

4. Know What to Do
   in Emergencies 13

5. Stay Alert Outdoors 16

6. Stay Safe Online 19

More to Explore   22

1 Play Safe Outdoors

Safety is important. Rules protect you and others from getting hurt. There are also safe practices. These are usually not written down. But following them keeps you safe.

When you are outside, you need sun protection. Wear sunscreen to avoid getting burnt. Drink lots of fluids. Water is best. If you hear thunder, go inside. A storm is close by.

In winter, dress in layers. Wear a hat and mittens to prevent frostbite. Wear warm socks and waterproof boots.

Did You Know?
When you play outdoors on a hot day, your body sweats. That's why you need water.

Protect Your Body

2

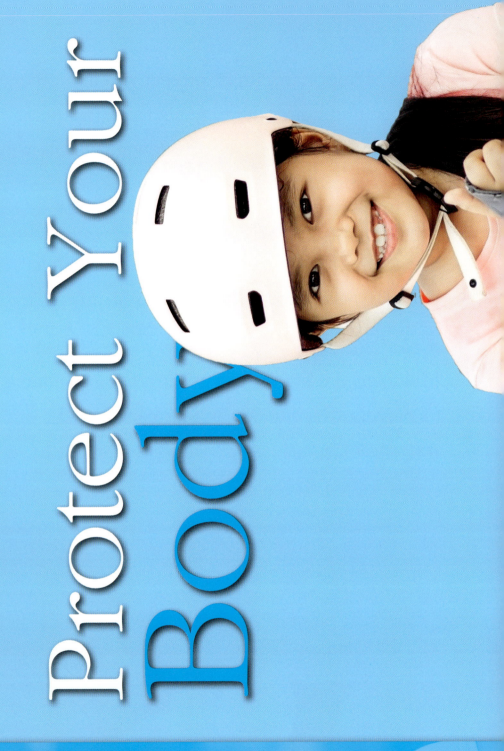

Before you get on your bike, scooter, or skateboard, protect your head. Wear a helmet. For scooters and skateboards, add elbow and knee pads.

Some sports require other safety equipment. This includes chest protectors, face guards, shin guards, gloves, and batting helmets. Learn how to wear them the right way.

Did You Know? Stretching before sports practices and games helps prevent injuries.

Stay Safe around Animals

3

Animals are cute. But they can be dangerous. They can bite and scratch. They can spread disease.

Stay away from stray animals. They are not used to humans and may hurt you. Ask before you pet other people's pets. Never get close to a wild animal, even if it is hurt. Instead, tell an adult.

Before you pet a dog or cat, let it sniff your hand. Move slowly so the animal isn't startled. And be gentle when picking up a pet.

Think About It
What would you do if a strange dog approached you? (Hint: Don't run.)

Know What to Do in Emergencies

Some emergencies come with a warning. What should you do if you hear a tornado warning? Go to the lowest place in a building. Stay away from windows.

What if there's an earthquake? Go to a room without windows, like a closet. Or crawl under a sturdy table.

Make a plan with your family. What if there is a fire? What if someone gets hurt? Write down emergency phone numbers. Keep this list in your backpack or on the kitchen fridge. You should memorize your parents' or caretaker's phone number too.

Did You Know?
Tornadoes can happen in any month. But they are most common from March to June.

Stay Alert

Outdoors

5

16

When outside, stay alert. Look both ways before crossing a street. Cross at corners and stay within crosswalks. Obey the "Walk" and "Don't Walk" signs on a stoplight.

Be aware of other people around you. Talk only to adults you know. Don't approach a car unless you know the driver. And never take a ride with a stranger.

It's always safer to go places with adults. But even with an adult, you can practice safe behaviors.

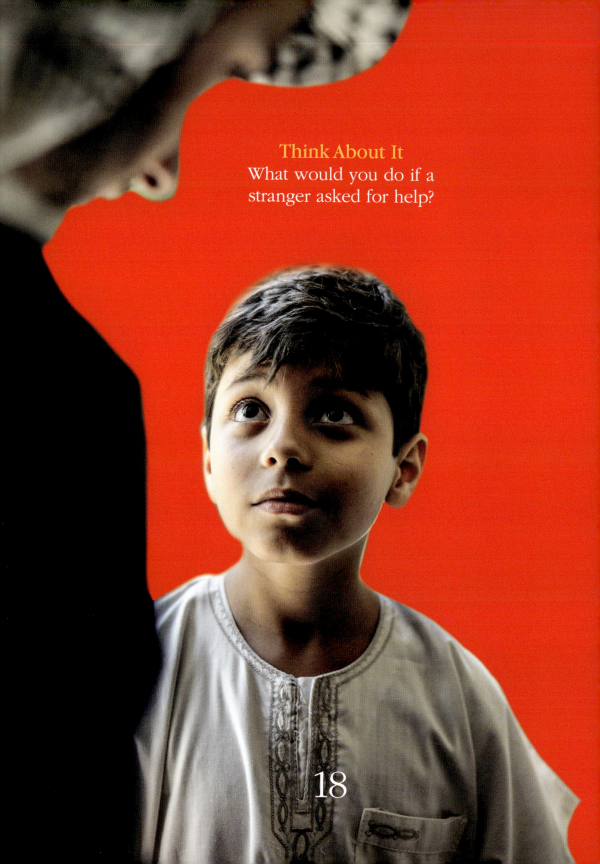

Think About It
What would you do if a stranger asked for help?

Going online can be fun and educational. It can also be risky for kids. Safeguard your personal information. Never give someone your name, address, or phone number.

Visit websites that start with "https." The "s" stands for "secure." Some good websites for kids are PBS Kids, MathGames, and National Geographic. Ask an adult before you download anything.

It can be fun to meet new people online. But it is also easy to lie or say mean things. Tell an adult if someone makes you feel hurt or uncomfortable.

There are kid-safe search engines. One is Kiddle. Another is KidRex.

Did You Know?

MORE TO EXPLORE
FANTASTIC FACTS

A helmet should cover your forehead. It should not tip back more than 1 inch (2.5 centimeters).

The sun is at its peak between 10 a.m. and 2 p.m. Make sure to wear sunscreen or stay indoors during these hours.

Most tornadoes occur in the central United States.

Most earthquakes within the United States happen in Alaska.

There are around 200 million stray dogs in the world.

At least 60 percent of kids in the United States use the internet at home. Some are as young as three years old.

MORE TO EXPLORE
COOL COMPARISONS

6 Dangerous Places and Activities: How to Stay Safe

PLAYGROUNDS
Don't push. Make sure equipment is for your age.

STAIRS & FLOORS
Be careful not to slip. Hold onto railings.

PLAYING SPORTS
Wear protective gear. Listen to your coach.

TRAMPOLINES
Take turns. Don't jump without a net.

RIDING BIKES
Wear helmets. Ride with an adult.

SKATEBOARDS & SCOOTERS
Wear helmets. Wear elbow and knee pads.

MORE TO EXPLORE
RESOURCES

Glossary
alert (uh-LURT) Being watchful and quick to act.
educational (ed-yoo-KAY-shun-uhl) Something that teaches.
fluid (FLOO-id) A liquid substance.
frostbite (FRAWST-byte) An injury to skin from freezing.
safeguard (SAYF-gard) To protect something.
startle (STAR-tuhl) To move or jump suddenly out of surprise or fear.
stray (STRAY) An animal that is lost or without a home.

Read More
Bassier, Emma. *Fire Safety*. Minneapolis: Cody Koala, 2021.
Ridley, Sarah. *Being Safe*. New York: PowerKids Press, 2022.

Index
animals, 11, 12
asking permission, 11, 20
being aware, 17
clothing, 5
internet safety, 20
safety equipment, 8
strangers, 17, 18
stretching, 9
sunscreen, 5
water, 5
weather, 5, 14, 15

TOP RANK is published by Black Rabbit Books, P.O. Box 227, Mankato, MN, 56002. • COPYRIGHT © 2025 Black Rabbit Books. All rights reserved. No part of this book may be reproduced in any form without written permission from the publisher. • Top Rank is an imprint of Black Rabbit Books. • Edited by Alissa Thielges • Designed by Danny Nanos • Photographs © Dreamstime: Creativefire, 19, Nigel Spiers, 14; Getty; FG Trade, 18; Shutterstock: Alinute Silzeviciute, 9, Andrey_Popov, 23, BearFotos, 4, ChutiponL, 20, Dmytro Zinkevych, 23, Ground Picture, 1, Jacek Chabraszewski, 23, kornnphoto, cover, 6–7, 8, maxitimofeev, 11, McLittle Stock, 13, Meike Netzbandt, 12, Monkey Business Images, 2, PaniYani, 16, paulaphoto, 2–3, Rasica, 15, Sharomka, 23, Susan Montgomery, 17, Tomasz Trojanowski, 23, vystekimages, 5, Zyn Chakrapor, 23 • Printed in the United States of America
Library of Congress Cataloging-in-Publication Data: Names: Snow, Peggy, author. | Title: Staying safe / by Peggy Snow. | Description: Mankato, MN: Black Rabbit Books, [2025] | Series: Top rank: healthy and happy | Ages 8–11 | Grades 4–6 | Identifiers: LCCN 20230582 | ISBN 9781632357991 (library binding) | ISBN 9781645820772 (ebook) | Subjects: LCSH: Danger—Psychological aspects—Juvenile literature. | Safety education—Juvenile literature. | Classification: LCC BF575.T45 S65 2025 | DDC 155.9—dc23/eng/20240129 | LC record available at https://lccn.loc.gov/2023058210